'Terry Waite sets his stories of mice families right in the present day . . . with television sets, even mice alarms (they're ineffective!) With a nod to his famous predecessor Beatrix Potter (there's mention of a tailor of Gloucester), his mice take on today's problems – rescue services, townies moving into the country property . . . and its all done with mischief and affection.'

Joan Bakewell DBE, writer and broadcaster

'A delightful set of tales from a master writer. Think you know Terry Waite's writing? Think again! Here, he delivers a book of captivating stories – tales with a golden heart – that are sure to delight young readers. What a treat!'

Paul Kerensa, comedian, scriptwriter and children's author

Terry Waite is best known as a hostage negotiator and a former hostage, having spent five years in solitary confinement. During those years he was denied pen or paper and so began to write in his head. Since his release from captivity in 1991, he has written several books but *Tales of Tommy Twitchnose* is the first one he has written especially for children.

The village of Cheesethorpe is based on a real Suffolk village and the old couple on friends of the author, Jenny and Alan, who live in a converted barn there. One day, Jenny and Alan returned home from holiday to discover that mice had eaten Alan's slippers! Jenny also found that they had feasted on horse chestnuts and left the shells in her bed! Thus Tommy and all his small animal friends were born.

Terry hopes that these stories will give those who hear or read them as much pleasure as they have given him writing them.

Tales
of
Tommy Twitchnose

TERRY WAITE

First published in Great Britain in 2020

Society for Promoting Christian Knowledge
36 Causton Street
London SW1P 4ST
www.spck.org.uk

British Library Cataloguing-in-Publication Data
A catalogue record for this book is available from the British Library

ISBN 978–0–281–08402–9
eBook ISBN 978–0–281–08403–6

1 3 5 7 9 10 8 6 4 2

Typeset by Manila Typesetting Company
First printed in Great Britain by Jellyfish Print Solutions
Subsequently digitally printed in Great Britain

eBook by Manila Typesetting Company

Produced on paper from sustainable forests

This book is dedicated to three young friends of mine who live far away in New Zealand – Hadyn, Laura and William

Acknowledgements

Special thanks are due to my editor Philip Law and all the staff at SPCK, who are always encouraging.

Jenny deserves a special mention for all her work on the draft copies, her helpful suggestions and for giving me her support.

Contents

1

The surprise visitors

Mr Tommy Twitchnose sat at his desk in his cosy little house under the floorboards of an old barn in the little village of Cheesethorpe. It was cold and raining outside but he was as warm as toast. The old couple who owned the barn had made it into a comfortable home for themselves and had put in electric radiators, which also heated Tommy's little den. He felt very happy. Some time ago, the old barn was falling down and his home was cold and damp. Tommy's wife, Tiggy, was always sneezing and his children had to wear tiny woollen jackets made from odd scraps of material he found in the farmyard. Now they were all warm and comfortable.

'Tommy, dear, are you awake?'

Tiggy Twitchnose was busy in her tiny kitchen, preparing a tasty supper of cheese and onion pie. She had found the cheese on the floor in the old folks' kitchen, where it had been left by a visitor who was always dropping food. When no one was around, she would scamper out of her front door and quickly gather what she could. One night it might be cheese. Another night some potato. There was always plenty to find as the old couple provided their visitors with lots to eat and some of them were careless eaters.

'Tommy, do come here,' urged his wife. 'I have something to tell you.'

Grumbling to himself, Tommy Twitchnose finished the letter he was writing and got up.

'Coming, dear,' he said and he scampered across the floor into the kitchen. 'What is it?'

'Don't sit there,' said his wife, as Tommy was about to sit in a chair made out of an old matchbox. 'It's too near the oven and you'll be in the way.'

Tommy was puzzled. If he was in the way, why had Tiggy called him into the kitchen? There was no telling but he said nothing.

'I have some important news,' said Tiggy.

She checked on her delicious-looking pie in the oven. Tommy's nose twitched when he saw the pie but he remained silent.

'Today, when I was visiting your cousins in the church,' Tiggy continued, 'I heard something very serious.'

Tommy's cousins were poor and had lived in the church for many years. No one ever dropped food there and the youngest mice always wore woolly coats, even in the summer.

Again, Tommy said nothing. He had learnt never to interrupt his wife when she was telling a story.

'News has got out,' continued Tiggy, 'that this old barn is a lovely place to live and a family of town mice are planning to move in very soon. Cousin Milly met one of them today. He was pushing a wheelbarrow piled high with furniture and he said they're coming here. We are going to be invaded, Tommy. Invaded! You must stop them!'

Tommy blinked and, quite forgetting himself, sat down heavily on the matchbox chair.

'Bless my whiskers,' he said. 'If town mice move in, the humans are bound to see them.

Town mice are so very loud and noisy and they will eat anything! Also they have no manners and make a mess everywhere they go. Oh dear, oh dear. What are we going to do?'

Tiggy Twitchnose gave her husband a gentle push as she went to open the oven door.

'Well, Tommy, it's up to you,' she said, and she placed the pie on the kitchen table. 'If you want a peaceful life, you'd better do something . . . Children! Supper's ready. Come along, Mike and Maggie. Quickly now!'

Two little mice appeared at the doorway and sat down with their mother and father. Suddenly, Tommy didn't feel at all hungry. He was busy thinking about how he was going to deal with this latest problem. It wouldn't be easy. Not easy at all.

Mr Daniel Dockmouse whistled to himself as he pushed his wheelbarrow along Church Road. Next to him scurried his wife Daisy.

4

She had been given that name by her father, who was a very important mouse in the London docks and was said to be friendly with the water rats. To her father's dismay, Daisy had married Danny, who had a small room in an old warehouse. Danny wasn't very important and Daisy's father was not at all happy when his favourite daughter married a common mouse from the London docks.

Daisy Dockmouse was carrying a large bundle on her back. Behind her scampered her five children, Sam, Susan, Sasha, Sheila and Billy. (The last one was called Billy because their father couldn't think of another name for a boy beginning with 'S'. Much later, he thought of Simon, but by then it was too late and so Billy it was.)

'How much further do we have to go?' asked Sam. 'I'm tired and I want my tea.'

'Will you stop asking me that!' said Danny rudely. 'Nothing but complaints from you lot. Smell the country air. The exercise will do you good. Step out smartly!'

As a young man, Danny had been in the Royal Mouse Brigade and had marched up and down the London docks under the supervision of the water rats. He was very proud of his old uniform, which was folded neatly and stacked in the wheelbarrow.

Suddenly, Danny stopped and the little procession behind him also stopped, bumping into one another as they did so.

'Good heavens,' he said, 'that's the place.'

Six heads turned and six pairs of eyes looked in the direction Danny was looking.

'It's a fine place to be sure,' he said. 'Just right for us all. Stay here while I have a closer look.'

The little family sat thankfully on a grassy verge while Danny walked up the long drive towards a fine-looking house. He walked around the back where he found an open door and slipped quickly inside. There was a delicious aroma of cooking and an old woman wearing an apron was standing by a stove preparing some vegetables. In a chair sat an old man. He was snoring loudly and looked very contented with his lot.

'Not bad,' said Danny to himself. 'Not bad at all.'

He was about to explore further when he heard a voice calling from a dark corner.

'Hey,' said the voice, 'what are you doing here?'

Danny turned and saw that it was another mouse speaking to him. The mouse was smartly dressed in a flat cap and a little shooting jacket.

'Hello, mate,' said Danny. 'Who are you? Off to shoot a few chickens, are you?'

'Shush,' said Tommy. 'You'll wake the old man and he can get very bad-tempered. Apart from that you don't shoot chickens. You shoot grouse.'

'Shoot what you like,' said Danny. 'As for being bad-tempered, I can get very bad-tempered. Especially when I'm hungry and at the moment I'm starving.'

'Well, you can't stay here,' said Tommy. 'I live here with my family and we've not found much food today as there have been no visitors.'

'Look, matey,' said Danny, putting his hands behind his brightly coloured braces and sticking his chest out, 'you might not know this, but you and I are related and I often said that one day I might pack up and leave London for the countryside, so here I am. This place is big enough for all the mice in the Royal Mouse Brigade and their relatives. Hold on while I fetch the wife and kids. Won't be long. This is just the place for us and we're moving in right now!'

Without another word, Danny slipped out of the back door.

Tommy didn't know what to do. There was no way he could stop the other family from moving in but it could make life very hard. There was only just enough food for his *own* family, let alone another one. He stood there in the corner of the old folks' kitchen, his nose twitching anxiously, a very worried mouse indeed.

'Anything I can do to help?' It was the familiar voice of the old man. He had got up and was now standing watching his wife prepare their supper.

'You can peel an onion,' she said. 'After that, what about collecting some bread?'

When he heard this, Tommy's ears pricked up. Bread, eh? The old man was bound to drop some on the floor and that would provide a good start to the family supper. He scampered across the hallway and into his house under the floorboards to tell his wife of their good fortune.

As he approached, he heard the most terrible commotion coming from his living room. When he entered, he couldn't believe his eyes.

The place was full of mice! He recognized Danny  Dockmouse at once. Danny was sitting in Tommy's favourite chair, munching on a piece of carrot, while several little mice children were

doing somersaults on his best carpet. Tommy's own children stood shyly in a corner looking on and Tiggy, his wife, was very flustered.

'Hello, Tommy, old boy,' said Danny cheerfully. 'Nice place you've got here. Great for grub too. In just a few minutes, me and the missus collected enough to last us all a couple of days, and plenty for you too. This is the place for us, Tommy, old fella. No doubt about it.'

Tommy was lost for words. He knew there wasn't enough room under the floorboards for Danny and his family unless he started major building work, and that would take several weeks.

Daisy, Danny's wife, was doing her best to get the children to behave. 'Billy!' she shouted to her youngest son. 'You are not to stand on your head on the sofa. Behave yourself. All of you.'

No one seemed to take any notice whatsoever and Danny continued munching his carrot.

'I don't want to be difficult,' said Tommy, as he glanced at his worried-looking wife, 'but there really isn't enough space down here. We only have one spare room and that's used by my cousin, the Reverend Albert Pew, when he comes to take a service in the church. Cousin Albert lives in Mousechurch and it's too late for him to go home after he's preached at the evening service.'

'What?' said Danny. 'A preacher, is he? That's about the only good reason I can think of for *not* moving here. I've heard enough preachers to last me a lifetime. A very pompous fella always took the annual service for the Mouse Brigade in London. At least he gave the lads an opportunity for a quiet nap.'

Tommy remained silent. He had no wish to argue with his town cousin.

Then, he had some sudden inspiration.

'I've just remembered something!' he said. 'Last week there was quite a palaver. A pack of travelling mice came by and settled down for the night in the old couple's bedroom. The humans didn't know the mice were there until they made themselves a couple of jackets from the old man's slippers and ruined them. This made the old man very cross so he set some traps. The travellers weren't so keen on that and they packed up and left. Anyway,  that must mean there's some space upstairs. It may be dangerous, though.'

'No problem!' said Danny boldly. 'There isn't a trap in England that I can't manage. You should see the size of the traps in the docks. Some were big enough to crush a water rat's car. As soon as it's dark, I'll go take a look. You can come with me if you like and I bet by tomorrow, we shall all be settled comfortable-like in the old chap's bedroom – traps or no traps! But now it's time to eat. Come on, Daisy!' he called to his wife. 'Hand over the grub to Tiggy and we'll all have supper together.'

After supper, Tiggy Twitchnose made up one large bed on the dining-room floor for the five children. She fetched some scraps of material from her store cupboard and sewed them together to make a duvet. Then she stuffed it with cotton wool to make it warm. Her own children had their own bedrooms, of course, where they slept under the same sort of duvet.

Before they all went to sleep, the children from both families sat quietly on the big duvet as both Tommy and Danny's wives read them stories from a big red story book that Tommy had been given when he was a boy. In it was the mouse children's favourite story of a big black cat named Tinker, who chased mice for miles and miles but never once caught one.

It made them shiver with excitement and laugh too as Tinker failed time and time again to catch even the slowest mouse.

Soon the children were asleep and the two mothers made their way back to the living room, where Tommy and Danny were chatting together. When they entered, Danny stood up.

'Right,' he said, 'Tommy and I are about to venture upstairs. The old folks haven't gone to bed yet. They're watching the television in the big room. Well, one of them's watching. The other is snoring loudly.'

Tiggy laughed. 'He sleeps in his chair every night,' she said. 'Sometimes he is so sleepy, he nods off at the kitchen table!'

They all laughed in a good-hearted way.

'All the better for us,' said Danny. 'Come on, Tommy, old man. Time for us to set off the traps!'

Slowly, the two mice crept out of Tommy's little home and made their way to the foot of the stairs.

'This is the dangerous bit,' whispered Tommy, as they prepared to jump up to the first step. 'If anyone comes out of the living room now, they're bound to see us.'

From across the hall, the two brave mice could hear a quiz programme playing on the TV, accompanied by the snoring of the old man in his armchair. But they managed to scramble up the stairs unseen and soon arrived at the door of the main bedroom.

'Pretty plush up here,' said Danny. 'Look at the carpet. Not bad, eh? We could be very comfortable in this room.'

The two explorers continued their trek across the floor.

When they'd got to the bedside cupboard, Danny let out a cry. 'Look!' he exclaimed excitedly. 'The crafty old man!'

Tommy was puzzled. All he could see was an electric socket with a plug attached to it.

'I don't see any trap, Danny,' he said.

'Look at this, my lad,' said Danny, pointing towards the plug. 'That's the latest device to scare you and me out of our wits, and our wives and kids too.'

Tommy was still puzzled.

'It's a clever little trick invented by humans,' Danny explained. 'When it's switched on, it makes a terrible high-pitched noise that only mice can hear. It drives you crackers. I saw many of these in London but, just watch, I'll show this old fellow that we mice aren't so stupid.'

'Do be careful, Danny,' said Tommy anxiously. 'Electricity is dangerous, you know.'

'Never fear,' Danny replied, as he fiddled with the device. 'I've seen many of these things and they can be dealt with in a jiffy. There!' he exclaimed. 'That should fix it.'

'What have you done?' enquired Tommy. 'It won't catch fire or anything like that, will it?'

'Not on your life!' Danny laughed. 'If that happened, we'd all be out of a home. No, it's something much better than that. You wait. I'll come back to this room tomorrow and we'll move in. You can be sure of that, Tommy, my friend.'

With that, the two adventurers set off back down the stairs to Tommy's home.

As Tommy was about to go to his bed, Danny turned to him. 'Sleep well, old chap. When you wake in the morning, I guarantee you'll have a real good laugh. You just wait!'

Then, he snuggled down in his makeshift bed and a puzzled Tommy went to his room.

That night, all the mice, except for Tommy, slept soundly. Tommy couldn't get to sleep for thinking about what was going to happen the next day. What had Danny done that would be so helpful to them?

He fell at last into a light sleep but was soon woken by a strange sound. Someone was coming down the stairs.

Tommy got up quickly and peeped out of his front door. The old man was slowly descending the stairs and, at the same time, groaning and holding his head in his hands. Then his wife walked across the hall with her fingers in her ears and muttering to herself.

Tommy was puzzled. Perhaps they were ill? He heard them boil a kettle and then go back to bed but he'd only been back in bed for ten minutes himself when he heard footsteps again. This went on all night and neither he nor the old couple got a wink of sleep.

The next morning, Tommy told Danny what had happened during the night.

Danny laughed. 'Ha!' he said. 'Just as I hoped. Come with me and we'll listen to what they're saying in the kitchen.'

The two mice left the safety of Tommy's home once again and hid themselves just outside the kitchen door.

'Oh, my poor head!' the old man moaned. 'It feels like it's splitting in two.'

'That's very odd,' said his wife. 'I have a splitting headache too. I haven't had a minute's peace all night.'

'I don't understand it,' said the old man. 'I can hear this terrible noise in my head. It's been there all night and it's still there now. It must be a fault in the wiring. Get on the phone right away and call the electrician. He set the system up. He can repair it.'

The old lady went to the phone, rang the electrician and explained the situation.

'All right,' the electrician replied. 'I'll come in an hour or so. Call-out charge seventy-five pounds and it's thirty quid an hour after that, plus the cost of materials.'

The old man groaned when he heard this but readily nodded to his wife to accept.

'Come on,' he said when she'd put the phone down. 'Let's go out and get away from this racket.'

Danny grinned. 'Just what we want,' he said to Tommy. 'When they've left, I'll slip upstairs and turn the machine back to how it was. That way, when the electrician comes, he'll find nothing wrong. I'll also look for a good place for us to live.'

The rest of the day passed peacefully enough. Danny's wife decided to take the children out to explore the countryside. Tiggy said she would go along with them and show them some of the sights of the neighbourhood. Tommy and Danny stayed behind to continue their plotting.

Later in the morning, the old couple returned and very shortly afterwards, the electrician arrived. The mice could hear him checking the plugs and sockets in the house, switching on lights and examining appliances. After over four hours, they heard him say to the tired couple that he could find nothing wrong at all and perhaps they were suffering from a bad virus that was going round the neighbourhood. He'd known several of his neighbours to complain of terrible headaches.

The old lady wasn't convinced. 'I'm sure it was an electrical sound,' she said. 'Quite sure.'

'Well,' replied the electrician, 'I can't find anything. By the way, my review of your system will cost two hundred and twenty-five pounds but, as I found nothing, I'll settle for two hundred cash.'

The old man went even whiter than he was normally but disappeared to his bedroom and returned with the money.

'There you are, mate,' he said, even though inwardly he didn't feel this man was a mate at all. 'I hope we don't have to call you back.'

The electrician left and the mice quickly retreated to Tommy's home.

'We shall have no more trouble,' said Danny. 'I'll slip upstairs later and switch the device back to how it was last night – but with one important difference: I'll turn off the sound completely. The light will glow and it'll look as though a noise is being made to scare us mice, but it won't be making any noise at all! If ever the old couple get difficult, I can always turn it on again to annoy them. Simple, Tommy, old chap. Now we can settle into our new home in the bedroom and both our families can be quite content and happy.'

And they were.

2

A happy Harvest Festival

Tommy Twitchnose was tired. For three weeks, he'd been out of bed as soon as the sun appeared in the sky. When he had dressed and brushed his whiskers, he collected a sack made by his wife from an old sock and set off towards the cornfield. It was nearly autumn and a busy time for the local farmers. The wheat they had planted months before had grown and ripened and was now being harvested. Huge machines called combine harvesters went up and down the fields, scaring the life out of the field mice who lived there.

Tommy scurried along Church Road with the empty sack slung over his shoulders. When he came to the gate leading into a field, he entered and went down a few steps by the side of the gatepost. There, hidden by some grass, was a little door. Tommy knocked on it three times.

'Come right in,' said a cheery voice, and Tommy lifted the latch and went inside.

'Hello, Cousin,' said a little fellow who was tucking into a large bowl of wheat flakes. 'Make yourself at home, Tommy. How about a bowl of wheaties? Plenty more where they came from!'

The little fellow was one of the field mice who lived in Cheesethorpe.

'Hello, Freddie,' said the weary Tommy. 'Today I think I will join you. It's my last day to collect food for the winter and I'm tired. It's a long walk from the old barn and back.'

Freddie Field Mouse smiled and took a little blue bowl down from the shelf. 'Here,' he said, passing Tommy the wheaties. 'We collected these last night and they are simply delicious. I have to stop myself eating them. If I don't, we'll have nothing left for when the cold days arrive.'

Tommy had just started to eat when, suddenly,

there was a terrific roaring sound and the whole house began to shake. He was so surprised that he leapt up from the table, scattering his wheaties all over the kitchen floor.

'Sit down, old fella,' said Freddie. 'Calm yourself. It's only the harvester passing by. It can't hurt us in this little house by the gatepost.'

Freddie Field Mouse fetched a small brush made out of soft rabbit fur and cleared up the wheaties. 'Have some more,' he said kindly, 'but be careful this time as the harvester will be back again soon.'

'I can't stay long,' said Tommy, 'but I wanted to see you because next Sunday we're having our great feast and you're all invited.'

Freddie looked puzzled.

'Have you forgotten?' asked Tommy. 'Next Sunday is the Harvest Festival in the church. It's the only time of the year when the church is full of food. The church mice are getting very excited. They normally collect enough food to last them for weeks!'

'Bless my whiskers!' said Freddie. 'So it is. How could I forget?'

'Easily,' said Tommy. 'That's why, when I've taken home my last sackful of wheat, I'm going round the whole of Cheesethorpe to invite every mouse family to attend. It's free. Another of our cousins, the Reverend Albert Pew, will come over especially from Mousechurch to take the service and, as soon as that's over, we'll all tuck in.'

'Splendid,' said Freddie. 'Really splendid. Next Sunday it is.'

With that, Tommy stood up, grabbed his little sack and made for the door. 'See you there, Cousin,' he said, 'eleven o'clock at night sharp!' Then he was gone.

Tiggy Twitchnose was busy. It was Sunday morning and she'd spent most of her time packing grains of wheat into small packages, which she stored neatly in a cupboard in her tidy kitchen. All the children were called on to help. The only person who was excused was Tommy, as he'd worked so hard every day to collect the food for the winter.

Every so often, they would hear heavy footsteps across the floorboards over their heads.

'Nothing to worry about,' said Tommy to Mike, his son, who was easily frightened. 'It's just the old man or his wife. They think that machine in the bedroom has scared us all away and have no idea we're here.'

Mike wasn't so sure. Once, when he was returning from school, the old man had spotted him running up the drive.

'Hey!' the man had shouted. 'Come quickly, Sally.'

The old man's wife came out to see what he wanted.

'It's a mouse!' shouted the man. 'We're being invaded again.'

'Don't be silly,' replied his wife, as she dried her hands on a tea towel. 'Calm down. There are always mice in the countryside. They won't harm you.'

'They ate my slippers,' said the old man. 'Goodness knows what they'll do if they get back in the house.'

'Come inside and have your dinner,' said Sally. 'Let the mice be.'

When the old man had gone indoors, Mike peeped out from behind the bush where he'd been hiding and crept quietly into his home.

Tiggy Twitchnose had laid the table and set places for all the family. When everyone was seated, she took her own place and looked at Mike and then at Maggie.

'Today,' she said, 'we will not have a large meal.'

The children looked disappointed. They always looked forward to their Sunday dinner.

'Also,' she continued, 'as soon as we've finished eating, we're all off to bed for an hour.'

At this news, the children looked even more glum.

'Don't you want to know why?' she asked them.

They nodded their little heads.

'Have you forgotten so quickly? Tonight is the great Harvest Supper in the church. We don't begin until it's dark and the church is securely locked for the night. Then, all the mice from miles around put on their best clothes and come to the service. Afterwards, there is as much to eat as anyone could want.'

At this news, the little mice clapped their paws together with delight and began to squeak excitedly. Tiggy smiled and served everyone with a small portion of toasted wheat flakes. Then, when the simple meal was over, they all went to their bedrooms and slept soundly until four o'clock in the afternoon . . .

It was getting late in the little house beneath the floor. Although it was dark outside, the mice's sitting room was quite cheery, as light from a lamp in the house above shone through a crack in the floorboards.

As they sat quietly, they could hear someone snoring and, faintly in the background, the sound of a television.

'Quickly now,' said Tiggy to the two children. 'Run along and put on your best clothes. We need to leave for the church very soon. Here, Tommy, let me help you with that.'

Tommy Twitchnose was struggling to tie a bow tie that the water rats had given him some years ago. His wife tied it for him.

'I think I shall wear my aunt's old bonnet,' she said. 'The church can be very cold at night and it keeps my ears warm. How the poor church mice live there, I don't know!'

Tiggy paused. Her nose twitched a little. Then she said, 'Tommy, dear, will you go and please get yourself a clean handkerchief from the bedroom drawer? Bring the red spotted one. It would go well in your top pocket.'

When Tommy had left the room, Tiggy drew the children close to her and whispered, 'Have you got the words?'

They nodded their little heads and said they'd both got a copy of the words in their pockets.

'Good,' said Tiggy. 'Now, be sure. This is to be a big surprise for your daddy and Uncle Albert, so don't breathe a word to anyone. Not one word.'

When the lights in the barn had gone out and all of Cheesethorpe was fast asleep, Tommy quietly opened his front door and the little group shuffled outside, their noses twitching in the cold night air. There was a bright moon in the sky, so they had plenty of light to help them find their way.

'Look at the moon,' said Tommy. 'That's called a Harvest Moon. Some people say it's made of green cheese but I don't believe that at all.'

Just as they left the front drive of the house and turned into the road, a great black shape approached them. Then another – and another.

The children let out frightened squeaks and held on tightly to one another. Tommy simply smiled.

'Don't worry,' he said confidently. 'It's only old Brock the badger out with his family for an evening stroll. Many animals only come out at night, when it's safe to do so. Evening, Brock,' he added cheerfully.

Brock gave a grunt and continued down the road.

As they got nearer to the church, they could see signs of great activity. Mice from all over the county were gathering for the big feast of the year.

Entrance to the church was through a tiny doorway just by the porch, and Cousin Albert, dressed in his best priestly robes, was greeting the mice as they entered. There was a lot of good-natured squeaking as mice who hadn't seen one another since the last feast exchanged greetings.

Suddenly, all went quiet as they heard the tinkle of a bell. A little carriage drew up outside the door, pulled by four dormice.

'That's Lord Whiskers of Whiskerton,' whispered Tommy to the children. 'He lives in the house of a real Lord and thinks, because of that, he is better than any of the other mice in the neighbourhood.'

The children stared as the rather grand-looking mouse stepped out of his carriage and raised his top hat to Cousin Albert.

'He says he is famous because his great-great-great grandfather was Mickey Mouse,' continued Tommy, 'but no one believes it except himself.'

As soon as Lord Whiskers had entered the church, the chatter started up again and Tommy ushered his family towards Cousin Albert.

'Why, hello, dear Cousin,' said Albert warmly, 'and you, Tiggy. How well you look and, my, how your two children keep growing! Come right in. I hope it will be all right for me to stay with you tonight after the feast, Tommy?'

Tommy nodded and Tiggy assured him that a bed had been prepared and all was ready. With that, they went inside.

The church was a sight to behold and the children couldn't believe their eyes. It was stacked from top to bottom with food of every description. Apples, pears, plums, wheat sheaves, potatoes, pumpkins. You only had to think of a fruit, vegetable or flower and it could be found somewhere in the church.

At the front sat Lord Whiskers, looking very pleased with himself. Next to him was his wife, who hardly ever spoke to anyone except to tell them off for something or other.

Behind them sat row upon row of mice from every corner of the county. There were mice in little sailor  suits from Volehampton; a large party of noisy town mice from Ratcastle; some rather well-to-do mice from the village of Nibblemore; and several solemn-looking mice who came from Shrewbury Prison. In fact, there wasn't one place in the whole county that wasn't represented.

Suddenly, the church went quiet and Cousin Albert, who was at the back, said in a loud voice, 'Let us sing from the *New Mouse Hymnal* hymn number 23.'

The special mouse choir, who came to the service each year from Twitchester, cleared their throats, and their musical director played the first few notes on his accordion. Then everyone began to sing...

> All things bright and beautiful,
> All creatures great and small,
> Apples, pears and apricots,
> We mice can eat them all.
>
> There's cabbage and there's onions
> And carrots by the score.
> There's bread and jars of honey,
> How could we want for more?

All things bright and beautiful,
All creatures great and small,
Apples, pears and apricots,
We mice can eat them all.

There's jars of pickled onions,
And oranges and dates,
And lots of ripe bananas,
And one or two iced cakes.

All things bright and beautiful,
All creatures great and small,
Apples, pears and apricots,
We mice can eat them all.

All things good and edible
Oh, what a lovely show.
And when the sermon's over,
We'll give them all a go.

All things bright and beautiful,
The church is full tonight,
We love Harvest Festival –
It is our favourite night!

By the time the hymn was over, the choir had walked to the front of the church and the Reverend Albert turned towards the congregation.

'Welcome, dear friends,' he said, in his best clergymouse voice. 'Once again, we are gathered to give thanks for this wonderful harvest. It's hard to believe that a year has gone by since we last met in this church. Sadly, some old friends are not with us but, happily, some new friends have joined us from London. Please will you stand, Daniel and Daisy and all your family.'

Danny Dockmouse, Daisy and the five children stood up and everyone clapped their paws together in welcome.

'Alas, not all is good news,' the Reverend Albert continued. 'I must beg of you to be well behaved. I have heard a complaint that an old gentleman's slippers were totally destroyed by one of this congregation.'

Tommy's nose started to twitch uncontrollably. He went hot all over and stared at the floor.

'You must all be very careful not to do things like that,' said the Reverend Albert. 'One dear friend lost his life by trying to eat an electric wire.

How sad and how silly. I want to see you all here next year, so please be good. Now, before the feast, we will sing our last hymn: number 48 in the *New Mouse Hymnal*.'

There was a rustling of pages as the mice turned to the correct hymn and the accordionist played the first line. Then they began to sing in their squeaky mouse voices:

> We search the fields and hedgerows
> For tasty things to eat.
> We're fond of new potatoes
> And quite like sugar beet.
> In winter when the snow falls
> And food is hard to find,
> Then all we have for dinner
> Is mouldy old cheese rind.
>
> All good gifts around us,
> They come from heaven above.
> We're part of God's creation
> And thank him for his love.

The Reverend Albert was just about to close the service when Tiggy jumped to her feet. Everyone stared at her. She turned and faced the whole assembly.

'Dear friends,' she said, 'tonight I have a surprise for you all and especially for my husband's dear cousin, the Reverend Albert. My two children, Maggie and Mike, have written a special hymn for him, which they will now sing to you.'

In the silence that followed, the two little mice scampered to the front of the church, holding the scraps of paper on which they had written their hymn.

Then they began to sing:

The day thou gavest, Lord, is ended,
Now is the time to go and rest.
The Reverend Albert has given his sermon
And we can all say t'was one of the best.

The Reverend Albert beamed and Tiggy wiped a tear from her eye as the whole congregation burst into loud applause. The two little mice returned to their places and then . . . the feast began.

By three o'clock in the morning, even though Maggie and Mike had slept the previous afternoon, their eyes were beginning to close. They were both full of good food and completely worn out from all the activities. There had been square dancing for the older mice and lots of games for the children. Maggie's favourite was musical chairs. As there were no chairs in the church suitable for mice to sit on, they had lined up a row of small crab apples and removed one each time the music stopped. Smaller mice kept rolling off them, which caused great amusement all round.

Eventually, the Reverend Albert picked a snapdragon from a display of flowers and, using it as a megaphone, he addressed the happy group.

'It is now very late,' he said, 'and soon we must be on our way home. But before we go, we have something important to do. Can any of the children tell me what that is? Not the big mice. You already know what we do every year.'

Lots of little paws went up as the children gave their answers.

'Eat more grapes,' said one fat little mouse.

'No,' replied the Reverend Albert. 'You've eaten enough!'

'Sweep the floor?' suggested another.

'That's a good idea,' said the Reverend Albert, 'but, as you see, the floor is quite clean and there's no mess. Does no one know?'

There was silence.

'Then I shall tell you,' he continued. 'All through the year, the church mice have a very difficult time as there is only food in the church during the Harvest Festival. Next year, that will change as the church is to open a café near the bell tower. But the church mice must have food for one more year until then, so we will now all get busy and collect as much wheat as we can to fill their store cupboards. Come on, let's get to work!'

Everyone jumped up right away and, in no time at all, the big store cupboards deep under the floor of the church were crammed full of lovely golden corn. Even the pompous Lord Whiskers filled his top hat with wheat and took that along to the store.

When the food collecting was finished, the Reverend Albert stood on a pot of honey and spoke for the last time.

'Well done, everyone. We must always remember to help one another and, of course, to enjoy ourselves. We have only taken a little of the food that's here and there will be more than

enough for the people when they come to church tomorrow. As we go home, let us all sing together our special mouse song.'

The accordion player struck up for the last time and they all began to sing:

> Hey ho, hey ho,
> It's back to home we go.
> We sleepy heads all need our beds,
> Hey ho, hey ho.
>
> Hey ho, hey ho,
> Into the night we go.
> The moon is bright and gives us light,
> Hey ho, hey ho.
>
> Hey ho, hey ho,
> Goodnight and off we go.
> See you next year, so never fear,
> Hey ho, hey ho.

With that, the mice darted out of the church into the bright moonlight and back to their homes beneath the floorboards and in the hedgerows.

UNDERGROUND RAILWAY - CHEESETHORPE STAT

3

Fun and games at a party

It was a perfect summer's day. Cheesethorpe was almost deserted. Nearly all the humans who lived there had gone away for their holidays and would not be back home for another week or more. This was the time of year when the mice and other little animals who lived in the countryside could walk around without fear of being seen.

Tommy Twitchnose was sitting in a deckchair on the grass outside the old barn, when he spotted Boris the tortoise, who lived in a very grand house at the side of the barn. Boris was a special favourite of the old couple, who made sure he was well fed and looked after. Like all tortoises, he was rather slow and, at the slightest sign of danger, could draw his head back into his shell and be quite safe. Tommy wished he could make himself safe like that. When danger approached him, he had to run for his life back to his home under the floorboards. Today, however, there was no danger and he sat enjoying the warm sunshine.

'What news, Boris?' he asked the tortoise, who had stopped by the side of the deckchair.

'Not much,' he replied in his slow way of speaking. 'The old man and his wife have gone away. They never take me with them but I don't mind. I like to walk around the garden.'

The garden was very large and the old couple had put a small fence around it so that Boris wouldn't wander into the fields and get lost.

'They like you,' said Tommy. 'We mice have a more difficult life. If they catch sight of us, they get scared and either run away or chase us.'

Boris gave a long, slow laugh. 'I've seen them,' he said, still laughing. 'I can run quicker than the old man and I carry my house on my back.'

Tommy nodded. He was glad he was free enough to run where he wished and, if he *was* spotted in the garden, he could always run down a tunnel dug by his other friends, the moles.

'You're lucky,' Boris said. 'I have to stay in this garden but you can go where you like. Are you off anywhere today? It's a lovely day for an outing.'

'Well, as it happens, we are,' said Tommy, as he got out of the deckchair. 'This afternoon, Lord Whiskers of Whiskerton is holding a garden party. All mice are invited for tea in the garden and a tour of the house.'

'Goodness,' said Boris. 'Whiskerton is miles away. It would take me weeks to get there.'

'Ah,' replied his friend. 'That's when it's good to be a mouse. All we have to do is pop down that hole over there.' He pointed to a hole by the side of the lawn. 'That is a secret entrance to a world humans know nothing about at all.'

'Well, I don't know about it either,' said Boris. 'Tell me more.'

'It would be useless to you, old chap, because you're far too big to squeeze down a hole in the ground, but we mice can do so easily. When we're ready, a mole wearing a little peaked cap greets us at the entrance and leads the way. It's as dark as night but that doesn't matter to the mole. Moles are almost blind but they can find their way without difficulty.'

Boris listened with growing interest.

'When we are about six feet down, do you know what we find?'

'Go on,' said Boris impatiently. 'What do you find?'

Tommy paused, as he was enjoying keeping the old tortoise guessing.

'Well,' he said slowly, 'if I tell you, you won't tell anyone else, will you?'

'Of course not,' said Boris. 'Please hurry up as I want to go and find some dandelions for my tea.'

'The moles are very clever,' Tommy said. 'Deep below the earth, they've made an underground railway that can take mice and their little friends to any part of the county.'

'Bless me,' said Boris. 'Who would have thought that! I've lived for more than eighty years and I never knew about such a thing.'

'Well, now you do,' said Tommy with a smile. 'Keep it to yourself, old friend. We don't want anyone else finding out about it.'

At exactly half past one that afternoon, Tommy and Tiggy Twitchnose and their two children, Maggie and Mike, walked across the lawn towards the secret entrance. They were dressed in their very best clothes. Tommy wore a real Panama hat, which had been given to him by one of the water rats when he returned from a very long journey to Ecuador. The water rat, who was extremely knowledgeable, told him that Panama hats were not made in Panama but in Ecuador, which was another country altogether.

Tiggy had a lovely purple scarf made from a scrap of silk that her aunt in Whiskerton had given her. The aunt lived in the silk factory and, although there was not much food, there were plenty of silk scraps, which she made up into scarves and dresses and sold to the mouse ladies of the town.

When the little family were halfway across the lawn, they caught up with Boris the tortoise, who had just returned from collecting dandelions.

'I'd give you a lift on my back,' he said to the children, as they overtook him, 'but I'm afraid I'm too slow.'

The mouse family all laughed.

'Thank you very much for your offer, Boris,' said Tiggy politely, 'but a walk will do everyone good.'

They left Boris behind and approached the tunnel entrance.

'Now,' said Tommy to the children, 'as this is your first time on the railway, I want you to be very careful. Do exactly what Station Master Mole tells you to do. The moles are proud of their railway and keep it very clean, so don't drop even one bit of rubbish. Not even the slightest piece. Understood?'

The children nodded their little heads and the whole family slipped carefully into the tunnel.

As they went deeper and deeper, the tunnel got wider and wider, and darker and darker.

'Oh dear,' said Mike, who was very timid. 'I don't like the dark. It's spooky.'

Just as he said this, they suddenly found themselves in a large underground cavern and all around them on the walls were hundreds of tiny glowworms, which gave the place a lovely warm light.

'Look!' cried Maggie. 'All our friends are here.'

Sure enough, the cavern was full of mice from Cheesethorpe.

'This is the Cheesethorpe stop on the Mousechurch to Whiskerton line,' said her father. 'No tickets are needed as the moles run this railway for all little animals to enjoy. They're happy to let us all see that life underground isn't as bad as some animals think.'

Maggie and Mike quickly caught up with their school friends and Tommy chatted with Danny Dockmouse, who told him that he was travelling alone to do some shopping. He and his family hadn't been invited to Lord Whiskers' party.

'You have to have lived here for many years before the old chap invites you,' said Tommy. 'He's not too bad but his wife would turn milk sour with just one look at it.'

Danny laughed. 'I don't care a hoot,' he said. 'Later, all my family will be going to the Grand Water Rats' Ball at the docks in London. That's a real do, I can tell you.'

No sooner had he finished speaking than there was the sound of a whistle and all heads turned towards the long platform at the end of the cavern. On a little stool stood an important-looking mole, wearing a peaked cap and holding a red flag.

'Dear friends of Cheesethorpe,' he began, 'I am the station master and I want to welcome you to my station. Today we're running a special train

to Whiskerton for those who are going to the garden party. There will be one or two other passengers but not many. Please remain seated on the train. Mind the gap between the train and the platform and have a happy journey. Here's the train now.'

Just as he'd finished speaking, there was the sound of a different whistle, and a little red engine pulling eight or nine open-top carriages drew into the station.

'All aboard!' shouted the station master and, quickly, all the mice on the platform settled themselves into their seats for the exciting journey to Whiskerton.

When everyone was on board, the engine driver gave another toot on his whistle and slowly the little train pulled out of the station. Maggie and Mike watched wide-eyed as the lights of the glowworms disappeared and, once again, they were plunged into darkness. Tommy, who had travelled on this train before, explained to the children that it was only the *stations* that were lit by the glowworms. The other parts of the journey would be in complete darkness and, as this was a special train, they wouldn't stop until they reached Whiskerton Station. Some of the mice in other carriages were quite frightened, so they began to sing. Soon, everyone was singing as the little train chugged its way along the track:

It's a long way
To see Lord Whiskers,
It's a long way
To go.
It's a long way to dear old Whiskers,
And the train is rather slow.
What's the use of worrying?
We'll get there in the end,
SO
It's a long long way
To see Lord Whiskers,
It's a long long way to go.

As it happened, the journey didn't take too long. The little train gathered speed and rushed through several stations, leaving many other animals standing on the platform. As they whizzed by, everyone on the train cheered, and those who were on the platforms waiting for a different train raised their hats and cheered back. They knew that this was a special train and they wanted the mice to be happy.

In no time at all, the train slowed down and another station master on the platform shouted: 'Whiskerton Station! All for Lord Whiskers' party, get off here. Whiskerton Station!'

Tommy and his family got out of their seats and made for the tunnel leading upwards. Mike and Maggie wondered what they were going to find next.

Lord Whiskers lived in a fine old house by the riverside. He had made a beautiful home for himself and his family in the cellar beneath the big house, which was home to a real Lord. Years ago, the cellar had been sealed off, so neither the real Lord nor his family ever went down there. This meant that Lord and Lady Whiskers were never ever disturbed and if they took care, they could come and go as they pleased. Today, as the big house was empty, they had taken over the garden and it was all made ready for the party.

Tommy and his family entered the garden, sat down in the shade of a rhubarb leaf and looked around. In one corner, a brass band was tuning up. A huge water rat had a bass drum strapped to his chest, two or three small rabbits were taking saxophones out of their cases and several mice were tuning up their different instruments.

'This promises to be very good,' said Tommy to his children. 'That is the famous Whiskerton Animal Brass Band and they are known all over the country.'

They didn't have to wait too long before a splendid-looking fellow in full uniform appeared, lifted his baton and the band began to play.

Tommy stared. There was something about this fellow that he recognized. Then the penny dropped and he couldn't believe his eyes.

'Bless my whiskers!' he said. 'Look, all of you.'

He pointed towards the conductor. Tiggy and the children stared at him.

'It's Uncle Danny!' said Maggie excitedly. 'It's Uncle Danny conducting the band!'

'It is indeed,' said Tommy, 'but what can he be doing conducting the Whiskerton band? I thought he was going shopping.'

The band continued to play and the mouse family continued to stare, wondering how it could be that Uncle Danny was doing such an important job.

Meanwhile, there was a buzz of excitement and all heads turned in the direction of the cellar. Lord and Lady Whiskers were walking slowly up the steps and into the garden. Lord Whiskers looked splendid in a grey morning suit and his wife wore an elegant long dress, together with an enormous hat that completely covered her face. As she always looked angry and often frightened the little mice, many of the grown-ups thought this was no bad thing. Some even joked that her look could freeze a bowl of hot custard at fifty paces!

When the splendid couple reached the centre of the lawn, the band stopped playing and Lord Whiskers looked round. Lady Whiskers remained hidden under her hat.

'Good afternoon, everybody!' he said in a loud voice. 'Today, my dear wife and I welcome you all to our garden party. I ask you to form an orderly queue in the refreshment tent, where there is plenty for everyone to eat and drink.'

Several small rabbits had made a tent out of beanpoles and rhubarb leaves, so it was a nice cool place to keep the refreshments.

'But first,' continued Lord Whiskers, 'before tea is served, we have some entertainment for you. Stand well back, everybody, stand well back.'

Lord and Lady Whiskers moved to the side of the lawn, where there were two little seats covered in silk from the local silk mill. They sat down and Lord Whiskers clapped his hands. Uncle Danny then raised his baton and the band struck up a rousing tune. As they did so, up from the river came six of the most amazing frogs anyone had ever seen. They cartwheeled on to the lawn and, right away, started to do backward somersaults, one after another. This was followed by leapfrogging over one another at an amazing speed. They finished their act by climbing on one another's shoulders and forming a tower, with the smallest frog perched right at the top. It was so exciting that the little mice covered their eyes in case he fell to the ground.

They needn't have worried. The little chap jumped down on to the soft grass and was quite unharmed. Then the frogs lined up, bowed to their audience and, as everyone clapped, they disappeared back to the river as quickly as they had arrived.

'Well,' said Tommy, 'those boys may look even worse than Lady W but they are very clever.'

'Shush,' said his wife. 'Don't be rude about your host.'

Mike and Maggie giggled but said nothing. Then, once again, Lord Whiskers and his wife moved to the centre of the lawn.

'I hope you all enjoyed that,' he said, and everyone cheered. 'Now, before we have our tea, there is one other act. This is even more dangerous and I want you all to be very quiet. Very quiet indeed. Look across there.'

He pointed towards a washing line that the real Lady who lived in the big house had put up to dry her clothes.

'Watch carefully,' he ordered, 'and don't make a sound.'

Everyone stared at the line. Out of the grass, there appeared a little red squirrel. He was wearing what seemed to be a pair of swimming trunks and carried a long pole. He bowed to everyone and, putting the pole between his teeth, he climbed up towards the line.

The drummer in the band began a roll on the drums and the bold squirrel, holding the pole on his paws, stepped on to the washing line. Everyone let out a gasp as the slack line began to sway from one side to the other, but the squirrel kept his balance. When he got to the centre, everyone gasped again as he threw the pole down on to the ground and remained swaying on the washing line.

Then, to everyone's amazement, the squirrel did a somersault and, before the audience could catch their breath, he quickly ran along the line to the other side. The audience burst into a loud round of applause as he bowed again, but the excitement wasn't over yet. The squirrel began to speak in a funny little squirrel voice.

'Thank you,' he said. 'My name is Red and I live here in the garden. Now, I would like to ask for a volunteer to come and join me.'

There was a buzz of excitement as the animals began to chatter among themselves. No one came forward. They were far too frightened to go up in the air with the squirrel, if that's what he wanted them to do.

'Oh,' said Red, 'I can see that you don't want to join me. Ah well, luckily I already have a volunteer.'

Out from behind a bush, a little mole appeared and he bowed to the group. The squirrel spoke again.

'Marcus here cannot see very well so he's not afraid at all. Come along, Marcus.'

Marcus jumped on the squirrel's back and, in a second, they were both at the start of the washing line, high above the ground. Everyone thought that Marcus was going to cross the rope on Red's back, but they were wrong. Red threw down a rope and, to everyone's surprise, hauled up a tiny wheelbarrow. Marcus jumped in and, very gingerly, Red began to push the barrow along the line.

Once again, everyone held their breath as, step by slow step, he pushed the barrow to the other side. When they finally reached the end, the whole audience stood up and began to cheer and cheer and cheer. They had never seen anything like it.

'What a lovely day, Mummy,' said Maggie, as the family sat in the cool refreshment tent enjoying their tea.

'It's not over yet,' said Tommy. He munched a delicious carrot that he'd dipped in cheese sauce.

Just before tea was announced, Lord Whiskers had asked everyone to make their way to the riverside once they had finished eating. There, Lady Whiskers would start the Grand International Vole Swimming Race. This important race took place every year in a different part of the country and this year,

Lord Whiskers was honoured that it was to be held in the river at the bottom of his garden. Voles were very fast swimmers indeed and some of the finest voles in the country had come to Whiskerton to compete.

'Quickly!' said Tiggy, as the children cleared their plates and Tommy finished his carrot. 'We don't want to miss anything.'

Along with all the others, they made their way to the riverside, where a large number of water voles had gathered. They each wore a swimsuit with the name of their team printed on the back.

'Look!' said Mike excitedly. 'There's the champion swimmer from Cheesethorpe.'

Sure enough, there he was on the bank, limbering up and getting ready to dive into the water.

The crowd gathered around and Lady Whiskers prepared to count down from ten and start the race.

'Ten, nine, eight, seven, six,' she counted, slowly and clearly.

The voles prepared to dive.

'Five, four,' she continued.

But just as she got to three, there was a sudden gust of wind and, horror of horrors, Lady Whiskers' large, decorated hat blew off and landed right in the middle of the river. She stretched out to catch it, lost her balance and, dear oh dear, fell straight into the water! Everyone let out a loud cry as she splashed about.

'Help!' she gurgled. 'I can't swim! Help! Help!'

Quick as a flash, before any of the professional swimmers knew what was happening, Tommy Twitchnose, together with Cousin Danny, jumped into the water and hauled the dripping Lady to the safety of the riverbank.

'Oh, my dear,' said Lord Whiskers to his wife. 'Are you all right?'

'Of course I'm not all right,' she replied angrily. 'I'm very wet! My clothes are ruined and I've lost my best hat. It's all your fault, Walter,' she said, addressing her husband. 'Take me home immediately.'

Lord Whiskers looked embarrassed as he took her by the arm and began to lead her up the lawn. Just before he left, he turned towards Tommy and Danny, both of whom were also dripping wet.

'Well done,' he said to the two brave mice.

Danny grinned from ear to ear, and Tommy's nose twitched proudly.

'You must come up to the house and bring your families with you,' Lord Whiskers continued. 'My staff will dry your clothes. Lady Whiskers will go to bed with a hot drink and then we will have a nice big supper together. After that, I will drive you home myself in my new Mousemobile.'

And that is just what he did.

4

A visit to the Houses of Parliament

'Why did you keep it such a secret, Danny?'

Tommy Twitchnose was sitting at home in Cheesethorpe chatting to his cousin Danny, who had moved to the old barn some time ago and set up home in the upstairs bedroom. Tommy had a house in the same barn under the floorboards and, in the evening, they often met for a chat together. Tommy was curious as to why Danny hadn't told him he was musical and would be conducting the band at Lord Whiskers' garden party.

'Well,' said Danny, 'I wanted it to be a surprise for you all.'

'It was certainly that,' replied Tommy. 'Where did you learn about music?'

Danny took a sip of blackberry squash before answering.

'Down in Greenwich,' he said. 'By the River Thames, there is one of the most famous colleges of music in the world and, under the ground floor of the school, the water rats have set up their own school of music. I used to go along to hear them when they played the Water Music at a concert or when they played for the Water Rats' Ball. They invited me to join them and that's how it all started.'

Danny must have had a real gift for music because he was very good and could play almost any instrument put before him.

'I was a judge when the Whiskerton Animal Brass Band came to give a concert in Greenwich,' continued Danny. 'They got first prize! So, that's the story,

Tommy. We London dock mice are not as stupid as some people think.'

'I never for one moment thought you were stupid,' said Tommy. 'Far from it. And what a night it was when Lady Whiskers fell into the river.'

'I'll never forget it,' Danny laughed. 'The water voles were lucky her sour looks didn't freeze the river over! Her old man isn't so bad but she's something else. I wonder what he has in mind for us?'

After the garden party, when Lady Whiskers had fallen into the river and was rescued by Tommy and Danny, Lord Whiskers had become quite friendly with the two mice. He would often drive over at night from Whiskerton to join them both for a chat, as he was quite lonely back at home. He'd said that he would call at around eight o'clock tonight and it was almost that time now.

In the house above them, the old man and his wife were watching a quiz programme on the television as usual. To be truthful, the old man wasn't exactly watching – he'd fallen asleep and was snoring loudly. Because of the noise he was making, his wife didn't hear Lord Whiskers patter across the floor and knock gently on Tommy's door.

'Come in, M'Lord,' said Tommy politely, as he showed Lord Whiskers to a comfortable chair. 'Tiggy and the children are staying with my wife's aunt, so Danny and I are keeping one another company.'

'Splendid,' said Lord Whiskers, 'splendid. But look, we've known one another for a while now. Why not call me Walter? I'd much prefer that. A good friend of my great-great-great grandfather, Mickey Mouse, was a man called Walter. Did you know that?'

Tommy and Danny shook their heads, never having heard of the man.

'Well, Walter was his name, although in America they called him Walt. I prefer Walter. But I didn't come here to talk about my relatives. I came here with an invitation.'

Tommy and Danny looked at him and said nothing.

'London is a long way away from here,' Walter continued, 'but I have to go every so often to attend the House of Mice. It's our parliament, as you know, and we have splendid premises right under the Houses of Parliament in Westminster. We've been there for years. Now, when I next go, I'd like you to come as my guests. I'm actually going tomorrow. Can you both make it?'

Their two faces lit up.

'You couldn't have asked us at a better time,' said Tommy. 'Both our families are away for a week so we can easily join you.'

'Splendid,' said Walter. 'Splendid' was a word he often used when he was pleased about something.

'Splendid. Tomorrow, both of you can join the Moles' Underground Express to London. I'll get on in Whiskerton and we can then travel together in comfort. I'll book your seats. All you need to do is get on the train. First Class, mind you. First Class all the way. Well, I must be off. Tomorrow it is. First Class, remember!'

With that, he slipped back out through the little doorway to his Mousemobile, which was waiting to take him back home.

Next morning, when all was still in the big house, Tommy slipped silently out of his front door. He'd packed a few things in a backpack and on his head was his favourite tweed cap. He also wore his very best winter coat, because he'd heard that the wind could be bitterly cold in London and he wanted to keep warm.

Very soon, he arrived at the secret entrance to the Moles' Underground Railway, where Danny was waiting. Danny was stamping his feet to keep them warm and didn't look too pleased.

'I thought you were never coming,' he said. 'I've been waiting here for ten minutes at least.'

'Your watch is never right,' said Tommy, who was a little bit cross at being told off. 'I'm exactly on time because I checked my watch by the Badgers' Broadcasting Company. Every few minutes that bad-tempered old badger – I forget his name – but every few minutes he tells us the time. So my watch is right to the second.'

All Danny could say was, 'Come on, then,' and the two travellers disappeared beneath ground.

As soon as they entered the cavern, which was still lit by hundreds of glowworms, the same station master whom they'd seen before walked towards them. In his hand he held two tickets.

'Good morning, gentlemen,' he said politely. 'I've been asked to give you these tickets with the compliments of Lord Whiskers. They're First Class tickets and if you stand at the end of the platform you'll be in the right place to get aboard.'

He handed them the tickets, gave a little bow and wished them a happy journey. Tommy and Danny had never been treated so well before.

'Not bad, eh?' said Danny. 'Hey ho, here comes the train.'

Sure enough, a little red train appeared out of the dark tunnel and stopped. Right in front of the two travellers was a carriage clearly marked 'First Class'.

'Here we are, old pal,' said Danny to Tommy. 'Off we go.'

The two little mice climbed aboard, closed the door and settled back into lovely, comfortable seats. They were off on their great adventure.

As promised, Lord Whiskers joined the train at Whiskerton and, as soon as he'd greeted his companions, he settled himself in a corner seat and fell fast asleep. For the whole of the journey, Tommy and Danny spoke in whispers, as they didn't want to disturb their host. All the way to London he slept. Then, just as the train was pulling into the station, as if by magic, Lord Whiskers woke up. He collected his umbrella and briefcase from the rack above his head and instructed his companions to follow him.

Lord Whiskers led them along several underground corridors in which lots of other little animals were hurrying about, intent on their own journeys. Eventually, they reached another platform, where they waited for a second train that would take them to the House of Mice. As they waited,

Tommy noticed a map on the wall. It showed all the train lines underneath the city and the names of the places where the trains went. Tommy put on his spectacles and looked more closely at the map. He saw that there were places called Barking, Blackhorse Road, Canary Wharf, Chalk Farm, Elephant and Castle, Ravenscourt Park, Shepherd's Bush, Warren Street . . . They sounded such interesting places and Tommy could just picture the different kinds of animals who lived there.

At last, the train they were waiting for arrived and they sat down for the final part of their journey.

'This will take us to the House,' said Lord Whiskers. 'It's a special train, run by the water rats.'

Within a few moments, the three mice from the countryside were stepping out of the special train and into the grand hall of the Mouse Parliament of Westminster.

'We are right beneath the House of Lords and the House of Commons,' said Lord Whiskers. 'They're a noisy lot in the Commons. Sometimes they shout so loudly that their voices can be heard down here under the ground. Now,' he said, without pausing for breath, 'wait here for a moment as I have to go and make arrangements for our security passes. When you have those, you will be able to go anywhere in the Mouse Parliament. Why not sit over there and make yourselves comfortable?'

He pointed to a long bench and the two mice did as they were told, while Lord Whiskers scuttled away. Five minutes passed, then ten, and Danny, who could be impatient, began to get restless.

'Where is the old fella?' he said to Tommy. 'If he doesn't come back soon, we'll see nothing. You stay here, Tommy, and I'll take a quick look round.'

'I think you ought to wait,' said Tommy, anxious not to cause any trouble. 'This is such a huge place, anything could happen.'

'Don't you worry, mate,' said Danny boldly. 'If anyone knows London, I do. See you in a few secs.'

With that he ambled across the hall and disappeared.

Danny was in an exploring mood. In the corner was a little door. He gently opened it and saw steps leading upwards. One by one he climbed them, up and up and round and round, until he came to another little door. He gently pushed on this one, scurried through and found himself in a very grand place. It seemed to be empty, so he had a good look around.

There were lots of green benches facing one another and on one of the benches was a big red box with the initials 'P. M.' in gold on the cover.

'I must be in the House of Commons,' he said to himself, 'and that box must belong to the Prime Minister.'

He was just about to explore further when he heard the sound of voices behind him. The only place he could hide was inside the red box so, quick as a flash, he jumped in and covered himself with one of the papers inside. To his horror, the voices came nearer. The lid of the box was snapped shut and Danny felt himself being carried off somewhere, then placed down firmly.

By now, even the bold Danny was quite frightened. He wondered how long he might be held prisoner in the box and what Lord Whiskers would say if he came back and found only Tommy. However, there was nothing to do but keep quiet and wait.

As he huddled there, he could hear the sound of people speaking. Sometimes there was loud laughter. At other times people were shouting, 'Resign!' or, 'Hear, hear!' or, 'Sit down, we've had enough!' Danny wondered what they were talking about. As he continued to keep his ears open, he felt the lid of the box move. He heard a woman's voice saying, 'I have the information right here for the Honourable Gentleman.'

At that moment, the lid of the box was opened and, seeing his chance, Danny took a tremendous leap and landed on one of the benches. As he did so, the woman who had reached for the paper let out a loud shriek that echoed around the whole room.

'A mouse!' she screamed. 'There's a mouse in my box!'

Everyone was so surprised by the shriek that they didn't hear her cry out about a mouse in the box. Some thought they were being attacked and ran out of the building. One person thought that the woman was having a fit and threw a jug of water over her. A voice was heard shouting time and time again, 'Order! Order! Orrrrrrr-derrrrrrr!' It was a dreadful scene.

In the middle of all the panic, Danny was able to scamper across the floor to the little staircase by which he had entered the room.

'Phew,' he said to himself, 'that was a near thing. I'd better get back to Tommy.'

He ran down the stairs and into the hall, where Tommy was still sitting alone. He had no time to explain what had happened, for as soon as he sat down, who should appear but Lord Whiskers, who was chuckling to himself.

'So sorry to be delayed, gentlemen,' he said. 'Business to attend to and a funny thing has just happened in the Commons. They say that the Prime Minister has gone completely mad and thrown all her papers up in the air. Whatever next! Come on, let's leave them to it. Now I'll show you a real parliament.'

With that, the little group went off for a tour that Tommy and Danny would remember for the rest of their days.

5

The Small Animal Rescue Service

'It's good to see you again, Cousin,' said the Reverend Albert Pew.

He was paying his monthly visit to Cheesethorpe to take the church service, after which he usually stayed the night with his cousin Tommy.

The two mice were now sitting comfortably in Tommy's home beneath the floorboards of the old barn. The children had gone to bed and Tiggy Twitchnose, their mother, was busy in another room.

'I remember when your children, Mike and Maggie, sang so beautifully at the end of the Harvest Festival,' said the Reverend Albert.

Tommy's nose twitched with pleasure. He hoped that his children would grow up to love music. All his family had been surprised to discover that Cousin Danny had actually studied at the Mouse School of Music in London. Tommy wondered if Mike or Maggie, or indeed both, might go there one day.

'But it's not music that I want to talk about tonight,' continued Tommy's other cousin. 'It's quite a different subject altogether.'

Tommy wondered what it could be. The Reverend Albert was a very wise mouse who had travelled all over the country and knew many small animals and birds. He often told stories of the animals he'd met and what they had done in their lives. Tommy waited to hear what was coming. He didn't have to wait long.

'Last week, I was in Duckbridge,' said Albert. Duckbridge was a small town near a place where a river flowed into the sea. 'I got talking to a seagull called Nelson. I know some seagulls can be very bad-tempered and greedy but this chap was quite friendly and was pleased to have a chat.'

'Wasn't Nelson the name of a sailor?' asked Tommy.

'It was,' replied Albert. 'He was a very famous sailor but he had only one good eye. Some small animals call the seagull Nelson because, like most birds, he has an eye on each side of his head, so when he looks at you it seems as though he is looking out of one eye.'

Tommy laughed. 'I'd never have thought of that,' he said.

Albert continued. 'He told me a story about a small bird called an Arctic tern. This little chap actually flew all the way from the north of England to Melbourne in Australia.'

Tommy looked puzzled. 'Where's Australia?' he asked.

Now Albert laughed. 'It's on the other side of the world, Tommy. Very far away. Look it up on a map sometime. But, my point is that when this little bird was there, he was told something that we might think about.'

Tommy listened carefully as Albert explained.

'In Australia, if one of the small animals becomes ill, a big bird will fly with it on its back to the nearest Small Animal Hospital. It's called the Small Animal Rescue Service. It saves so much time. The friendly seagull has offered to do the same for us here in Cheesethorpe and I think you, Tommy, should be in charge.'

'Me?' said Tommy. '*Me?*'

'Yes, you!' replied the Reverend.

'But I've never flown in my life,' said Tommy. 'I don't even know this seagull.'

'Don't worry about that, Tommy,' said his cousin. 'Tomorrow I'll introduce you to him and you can have a test flight.'

Tommy remained silent. Flying wasn't something that he thought he would ever do. Often, he'd seen birds flying high in the sky and wondered what it would be like to look down on Cheesethorpe. Now he had a chance to fly himself but, to be truthful, he was a little bit frightened.

Tommy didn't sleep too well that night. He dreamt that he was falling out of the sky, and the dream scared him. He seemed to fall and fall and fall and, just before he hit the ground, he woke up with a start.

'Phew,' he said to himself. 'That was awful.'

'Tommy,' pleaded his wife, who had also woken up, 'do please be quiet.'

Tommy hadn't told Tiggy about the test flight the next day as he didn't want to worry her.

'Sorry,' he said, 'I must have been dreaming.'

'You've been dreaming all night,' complained Tiggy. 'It must be the cheese you had for supper.'

Tommy said nothing but turned over in bed. He didn't sleep again and was wide awake when he heard the old man walk across the floor above him. Time to get up.

It was a lovely sunny morning and a special day for the small animals who lived in Cheesethorpe – the day of the parish picnic. This year, the Reverend Albert had arranged for there to be a special coach to take everyone to the seaside. They all had to bring their own food and would share it with one another when it was time to eat.

Tommy still hadn't told anyone about the seagull and the test flight he was going to take that morning, as he didn't want to cause worry and spoil anyone's day.

Before breakfast, Tiggy had been busy preparing a picnic, while Mike and Maggie found their sun hats and also a bucket and spade for making sandcastles. When they were ready, the Reverend Albert spoke to the children.

'The coach will be here soon,' he said, 'and you can travel on it with your mother. Your father and I will come along later, as there are one or two matters we need to discuss. We will meet you at the picnic spot by the seaside later this morning.'

Maggie and Mike were so excited that they jumped up and ran outside to wait for the coach. When it arrived, they got on with their mother and waved goodbye.

Tommy and the Reverend Albert went back to the garden.

'We'll go right to the far end by the trees,' said the Reverend. 'The old man and his wife won't see us there. Nelson said that he would be here at about half past nine. Come along, it's almost that time now.'

The two mice scampered through the long grass by the side of the garden until they came to the trees. They had just arrived when they heard a beating of wings and a huge seagull landed right beside them. Tommy felt very frightened to be standing next to such a large creature, but the bird seemed friendly enough.

'Hello, Rev.,' the seagull said, in what seemed to be a very loud voice.

Before the Reverend could answer, the seagull looked at Tommy. 'You must be Tommy,' he said. 'I've heard a lot about you. My name is Nelson and I fly everywhere. Over the sea. Over the land. I don't mind. Today, old chap, you will fly with me. Look here.'

The seagull walked towards a tree and pulled out a little package from behind a door that Tommy had never noticed before.

'This cupboard was given to me by an old woodpecker who used to live here long ago,' said Nelson. 'It's very useful as a storage place.'

He pulled out a little flying helmet and handed it to Tommy.

'Put that on, and here is your flying jacket.'

Tommy put both of them on and felt very snug and warm.

'Once we're up in the air, it'll get cold,' said Nelson. 'That's why I have all these feathers. They keep me warm. Right. All you have to do is hop on my back and hold tight. Are you ready?'

Albert gave Tommy a hand to clamber on to the back of the seagull and Tommy held on tightly to the feathers, his nose twitching nervously.

'There's a belt in front of you,' said Nelson. 'Fasten it tight and you'll be quite safe.'

Tommy did as he was told and, as soon as the belt was fastened, the seagull started to run. Within a moment, Tommy was flying through the air, higher and higher and higher.

At first, Tommy kept his eyes tightly closed as he was too scared to look down.

'If you look down, you'll see the road to the seaside,' squawked Nelson. 'Soon we will follow that, but before we do, I will take you on a little tour of Whiskerton, so you can see what it looks like from the air.'

Tommy slowly opened his eyes and, far below, he could see a road winding through green and yellow fields.

'That yellow colour is rapeseed,' said the seagull. 'It smells awful but they make it into cooking oil.'

The whole countryside below looked just like the patchwork quilt that Tiggy Twitchnose had made some time ago. Soon they saw a sparkle of blue.

'That's the river,' said Nelson, after they had flown all around the countryside. 'If we follow it, we'll come to the seaside and perhaps see your family. That would surprise them!'

'It would indeed,' said Tommy to himself and he clung even more tightly to the seagull.

'I'm going to follow the road that leads to the sea,' said Nelson, as he flew onwards. 'That way, we might be able to see where the coach is parked and so find your family. Hold tight, Tommy, I'm going down lower.'

Slowly, the ground came nearer and nearer, and Tommy could see the sea in the distance. He let out an excited cry.

'The sea, Nelson! The sea! I can see the sea!'

'It's good, isn't it?' replied the seagull. 'When I see the sea, I always feel quite at home.'

The sea came closer and closer but there was no sign of the coach or the little group that had gone for a picnic.

'Don't worry,' said Nelson to Tommy, who was looking for them anxiously. 'They may be a little further along the beach. I know the place where coaches often stop and that's where we're going now. I'll fly quite low, Tommy. Keep holding tight.'

Tommy didn't need to be told to hold on. He was still quite frightened, although he was just beginning to enjoy the experience.

He was looking out across the sea at a small boat bobbing up and down in the water when he heard Nelson cry out, 'Tommy, did you see that?'

Tommy had no idea what Nelson was talking about. 'Do you mean that little boat?' he asked.

'No,' replied Nelson. 'I mean over there, by those rocks.'

The seagull swooped low across the sand. 'Look there,' he said.

Tommy looked hard, then let out a cry of surprise. 'Goodness! It's a little mouse in trouble. He's waving a red handkerchief.'

'Hold tight,' said Nelson to Tommy. 'I'm going to land.'

The seagull stretched his wings out as wide as they would go and, in a few moments, they had landed quite gently on the sandy beach. Tommy kept his eyes on the little mouse, who, when he saw the huge bird landing close by, ran for all his worth and hid behind a large rock. Tommy then undid the safety belt and slid off the seagull's back.

'That little mouse is in trouble,' he said to Nelson. 'I'll go to see if I can help. Don't leave without me.'

Tommy had no time to remove his helmet and long coat and if he could have seen himself, he would have realized that he looked quite scary. He climbed over the rocks and cried out, 'Hello, little chap. Where are you? Don't be afraid.'

A little head popped out from behind a rock and let out a loud squeak of fright at the sight of Tommy, before disappearing again.

'Come on, young fella,' said Tommy. 'No need to be scared. It's only me, Tommy Twitchnose.'

As soon as he'd said this, the little head appeared once again and this time it was Tommy who let out a loud squeak of surprise.

'Mike!' he said. 'What on earth are you doing here?'

'Daddy,' replied the little mouse, 'is that really you?'

Tommy took off his helmet so he could be seen clearly.

'Of course it is,' he said. 'Look. But tell me, what are you doing here and where is everyone else?'

Mike began to cry. 'I was doing some exploring,' he sobbed, 'when I was chased by a big black dog. I squeezed into a little cave and had to wait for ages until the dog went away. When I came out, I was so frightened that I forgot my way back to the others. Oh, it was awful,' he cried, 'really awful. I waved my red handkerchief, hoping that someone might see me.'

'Well, that was exactly the right thing to do,' said Tommy with a smile. 'I saw you from way up in the sky.'

Mike stopped crying. 'What do you mean?' he asked.

'Follow me, Mike,' Tommy said. 'You'll find out in a minute.'

Tommy took his little son by the hand and together they walked towards Nelson, who was standing quite still looking out to sea.

'We have another passenger,' said Tommy, as they approached the seagull. 'This is my son Mike. He was lost.'

'Well, well, well,' squawked Nelson. 'Would you believe it? Jump on board, then, and we'll find your family. You can tell me the whole story later.'

Tommy put on his helmet and tied the red handkerchief around Mike's head.

'That'll have to do for the moment,' Tommy said. 'Come on, Mike. You sit in front of me and I'll hold you tight. We'll soon find the others.'

Tommy was not at all frightened now but little Mike was shivering with fear.

'Just close your eyes and hold tight,' said Tommy.

When Nelson had checked that they were both secure, he once again did a little run across the beach and soared into the sky. Mike hid his head in Nelson's feathers but Tommy, who was by now quite used to flying, kept a look out for the coach and his family.

They had only been flying for a few minutes when Nelson called out, 'There they are. Look!'

Tommy could see them now, but it didn't look as though anyone was having a picnic. Instead, he saw lots of little animals scurrying around and, even though he was up in the sky, he could hear them calling out, 'Mike, Mike, where are you? Mike! Mike!'

Once again, the seagull swooped low over the sand. This time he landed by the side of a small rock so that it was easy for Mike to step down.

'I'll leave you now,' said Nelson. 'I want to do some fishing while I'm here. They'll find a space for you both on the coach, I'm sure. Goodbye for now, Tommy. Leave the coat and helmet in the cupboard when you get home. We'll need them again when there's an emergency. Toodle pip!'

With that, he did a little run and soared away into the sky and over the sea.

6

The very naughty squirrel

Tommy Twitchnose, his cousin Danny and their two wives, Tiggy and Daisy, were sitting together in the big garden. The old couple who lived in the converted barn had gone away to the other side of the world for three whole months, so the small animals had the garden to themselves. Tommy, in his little house under the floorboards, had heard the old woman tell her husband to please get on with his packing as, if he didn't, she would go without him and leave him to cook for himself. Tommy wished that would happen as the old man was rather careless and would drop plenty of food on the floor, which would keep Tommy and his family quite happy.

In the end, the old woman did all the packing for both of them and, when the couple were ready, all the small animals who lived there came out and waved them goodbye. The old people never saw them, of course, as they were far too busy talking to the driver of their taxi.

As soon as the taxi had driven away, Tommy and Danny brought out a small table and chairs so that all four of them could have tea. As they were chatting and relaxing in the warm sunshine, they heard a beating of wings and who should land beside them but Nelson the seagull.

'Hello,' he said cheerfully. 'Anything left for me?'

Tiggy gave a big smile. 'You're in luck, Nelson,' she said. 'I've just made some fish paste sandwiches and you can have as many as you like.'

Ever since Nelson had rescued Mike on the beach, Tiggy was always glad to see him. Although seagulls can be greedy birds and gobble everything up, Nelson was very well behaved and only took what he was given.

'Thank you,' he said, as Tiggy handed him a large sandwich. 'I'm glad to catch you at home as it's you I wanted to see.'

'Me?' exclaimed Tiggy. 'Why do you want to see me, Nelson?'

'It's about the Small Animal Hospital,' Nelson replied in his funny seagull voice. 'We have to find a way to keep it going. When we opened the hospital, the water rats in London gave us a lot of money but they can't help us for ever. The other day, the hospital board met and decided that we ought to open a shop to help raise more money. As Tommy will soon be taking up his position as Chairman of the Board, we thought that you, with some helpers, might run the shop for us.'

Tiggy looked surprised as she'd never done anything like that before in her life. She looked at Danny's wife, Daisy, who was helping herself to a slice of carrot cake.

'Would you help me, Daisy?' she asked.

Daisy blinked. 'Well,' she said thoughtfully, 'I did run a vegetable stall when we lived in the London docks so, yes, I could give you a hand.'

'Well done,' said Nelson, as he gave a flap of his wings

that almost sent the tea table flying. 'If you want, you can jump on my back and I'll take you to see the place we have in mind.'

Tiggy stopped smiling. 'Thank you, Nelson, but no,' she said. 'I would be far too scared to do that. Just give me directions and tomorrow we'll all come to see.'

'Righto,' said Nelson, cheerfully. 'I'll get directions sent to you tonight. See you tomorrow. Toodle pip!'

With that, he did a little run and soared high into the sky. Little did Tiggy realize that she and her family were about to have an adventure such as they had never had before.

No sooner had Nelson flown away than the little group heard the tramp of feet as someone came up the drive. He was wearing a smart blue uniform and was pushing a bicycle.

'Why, Constable,' said Tommy, getting up out of his seat. 'Good to see you. Come and join us for a cup of tea and a piece of cake.'

Constable Charles Catchem was the local policemouse for Cheesethorpe, but because he had to cover such a wide area on his bicycle, he was rarely seen in the village.

'Thank you, Tommy,' he said politely. 'Good afternoon to you all.'

Danny had brought out a large chair because Constable Catchem was a very tall mouse and rather plump also.

'Ah,' he said, as he sat down, 'it's good to have a short rest. I have to push my bike quite a lot through long grass and these boots do hurt my feet at times.'

The policemouse took a sip of his tea. 'Now,' he said, 'you may wonder why I've come to see you this afternoon. Well, I'm here to give you a warning.'

At this, everyone began to look serious. Danny wondered what he might have done wrong in the last few weeks but could think of nothing.

The constable could see that he was uncomfortable and continued. 'Nothing to worry about,' he said, 'but you need to be on your guard. You know, when we first join the police, we policemice are told that we must keep two points in mind: protection and prevention. The two Ps.'

Tommy gave a quiet sigh. In the past, Constable Catchem had been to Cheesethorpe to give a talk to the small animals. They had gathered in their meeting room under the village hall and he had lectured them for over an hour. Tommy hoped that the lecture in the garden would not be as long as that.

'The two Ps are very important to us policemice,' Constable Catchem continued. 'Protection and prevention. We are here to protect all small animals from those who would harm them and we also are here to prevent anyone from doing wrong things. I'm sorry to tell you that here, in Cheesethorpe, someone has been up to no good. No good at all.'

The little group listened carefully and PC Catchem went on with his story.

'Here in Cheesethorpe, several families have reported things as missing, believed stolen. The church mice had their larder broken into. Someone else had a whole basket of clean washing stolen. We policemice have an idea who might be doing this, but we have no proof yet, so all I can say is, please be on your guard. If you see anything suspicious, tell me right away. Well, I must be off.'

Everyone stood up and Tiggy handed the policemouse a large slice of carrot cake wrapped in a green leaf and neatly tied with a piece of dried grass.

'Much obliged I'm sure, ma'am,' said PC Catchem politely. 'Keep a sharp look out and lock your doors at night. Good afternoon to you all.'

Then he collected his bicycle, which he'd propped up against a low bush, and pushed it slowly down the long drive.

Later that evening, just after Tiggy had put her two children to bed, there was a gentle knock on the door. Tiggy opened it and there stood a tiny dormouse, carrying a small envelope.

'Mrs Twitchnose?' he squeaked.

'That's right,' she replied. 'Would you like to come in?'

'No, thanks,' he said. 'I must get home as I have to get up early in the morning to go to school. Nelson the seagull asked me to give you this message.'

'Well, thank you very much,' replied Tiggy, 'and please thank Nelson also. I think I know what it is. Keep safe and get along home quickly. Goodbye.'

The dormouse gave a little bow because he was very polite, then scampered away down the long drive.

Tiggy opened the envelope and found what she thought she would: directions to the new shop. The shop was within easy walking distance so, the very next morning, she went to inspect her new place of work. She scurried along the drive, out into the road and headed towards the church, just as the directions said.

When she got near the church she stopped. There, in a small hole in the wall, was a lovely little shop. It had a large window full of small jars of honey that the local bees had given to help the shop get started. She was just about to go inside when she heard a flapping of wings, and Nelson the seagull landed beside her.

'Hello, Mrs Twitchnose,' he squawked cheerfully in his funny seagull voice. 'Our other helper, Doris, should be inside sorting things out. Let me introduce you. Doris!' he called out. 'Mrs Twitchnose is here to see you.'

A small, kind-looking dormouse came to the doorway. She was wearing a neat apron and around her shoulders was a beautiful multicoloured scarf.

'Hello, my dear,' she said to Tiggy, in a gentle voice. 'I'm so pleased to see you. The past few days have been very busy as all the available dormice in Cheesethorpe have been setting up the shop and collecting things for us to sell. Come inside and I'll show you round.'

'Well, I'll be off,' interrupted Nelson. 'Toodle pip!' Without another word, away he flew.

'Nelson has told you my name, hasn't he?' asked Doris, when Nelson had left. Before Tiggy could reply she continued, 'He's such a help but no use at all in setting up the shop. He's too big and clumsy. The dormice have been wonderful. Look.'

Tiggy went inside. Her nose twitched in amazement at all the wonderful things on sale. There were sweets and nuts and baskets of fruit; there were little wooden toys and games; there were hats and scarves and a whole rack on which hung colourful jackets to fit all sizes.

'My,' said Tiggy, as she looked at the jackets. 'Aren't they beautiful!'

'We're lucky to have them,' replied Doris. 'A very skilful mouse who lived in Gloucester gave them to us. He was a tailor and, when he retired, he gave all his expensive stock of clothes to help the hospital.'

'I'm a bit puzzled,' said Tiggy, as the two of them sat down to have a cup of tea. 'Nelson said that I was to be in charge of the shop but it's clear that you've done all the work and it's you who ought to be the manager.'

Doris Dormouse blushed. 'Well, dear, I have to admit, I have done a lot of work but . . .' And here she stopped and looked embarrassed.

Tiggy didn't say anything but waited for Doris to continue.

After a few moments, Doris went on. 'You see, my dear, I was never very clever at school. Maths always had me totally puzzled and, even today, I can't really add up properly. I had to tell Nelson this and he was very kind. He said he would ask you to take care of that side of things and be in overall charge, but you wouldn't need to be here every day.'

Tiggy put her arm round her new friend. 'Don't worry at all,' she said in a gentle voice. 'That will be fine. I can look after the money and you will be the shop manager.'

'Oh, thank you so much, Tiggy,' replied Doris, with tears in her eyes. 'I felt so ashamed at having to tell you that.'

'There's nothing at all to be ashamed of,' said Tiggy. 'One day, I think we might start some classes for older mice who had difficulty at school. Until then, I'll do just what's needed. We'll begin tomorrow.'

The next morning, Tiggy arrived at the shop early and discovered that Doris was already sorting through a basket of odds and ends someone had left outside the door during the night. There were one or two small ornaments, an old clock and several patterned plates.

'My goodness, Doris,' said Tiggy, when she walked through the door, 'you do start early, don't you?'

Doris looked shyly at her. 'Well, I do like to get things sorted out before people come in to look round. Also, we need to put the price on each item. It does take time, you know. Let's get this rack of coats outside. Animals will stop to look and they might even try one on.'

The two mice took hold of the rack and wheeled it outside the shop. The bright colours of the coats were most attractive and anyone passing would be sure to stop and look at them, and possibly be tempted to come into the shop and look round.

When the rack was in place, they went back indoors and Doris picked up the basket that was full of bric-a-brac. The price was clearly marked on each item.

'There,' she said. 'We might have some good sales today. People will be curious to explore a new shop in Cheesethorpe.'

Sure enough, it was very busy that morning. Several moles came in and rummaged through a box of old sunglasses. The bright sun, they explained, was too much for them. They were happier underground but they had to come to the surface from time to time, so sunglasses were a great help.

Two or three water voles came in together too and looked through a box of new swimming trunks that the tailor had given to the shop when he retired. A red squirrel, who was passing through Cheesethorpe on his way to see his friends in Pawminster, stopped and bought some chocolate nuts as a gift for them. It was a very busy morning indeed. By lunchtime, the two shopkeepers were tired and decided that they would close the shop for a couple of hours so they could have a sandwich and a little rest.

They went outside to bring in the rack of clothes and the basket of bric-a-brac but, to their surprise, there was no basket.

'Are you sure you didn't bring in the basket, Tiggy?' asked Doris when they had got the rack indoors.

'No, I didn't,' said Tiggy. 'When I last went out, it was still there.'

'Well,' said Doris, 'it's not there now. Someone has taken it without paying. How could they be so mean as to take money away from the Animal Hospital?'

They were both feeling very sad, when they heard a flapping of wings outside and a solemn voice called out, 'Ladies, can I have a quiet word with you?'

At first when they heard the sound of wings, they thought it might be Nelson but the voice was quite different.

They got up and went outside, and who should they see but Barney the barn owl. Barney was hardly ever seen in the daytime as it was then that he would perch high up in the branches of a tree and go to sleep. He would sometimes wake up but usually he was only out and about at night.

'Hello, Barney,' said Tiggy. 'I'm surprised to see you at this time of the day.'

Barney blinked his big wide eyes and looked at them seriously. 'I should be asleep but I have something very important to tell you,' he said. 'This morning, I was sleeping in the oak tree right opposite your shop. At about half past twelve, I woke up – and do you know what I saw? A little grey squirrel was coming along the road. He looked very shifty. He stopped outside your shop, looked at a basket, picked it up and, quick as a flash, ran with it down the road and disappeared up a tree.'

'My goodness,' said Tiggy. 'That squirrel must be the thief Constable Catchem is looking for. We must call him right away. Thank you so much, Barney.'

Barney blinked again. 'It's a pleasure but I must go back to sleep now. Nelson has asked me to keep a watch on your shop all night and I don't want to miss the thief if he comes back when it's dark. Good day, ladies, good day.'

He fluttered off, back to his perch high up in the oak tree.

A little while later, Police Constable Catchem could be seen at the end of Church Road, peddling as fast as he could on his bicycle. By the time he reached the little shop, he was quite out of breath. He went inside and almost bumped his head on the ceiling. If he'd kept his helmet on, he wouldn't have been able to stand up straight at all.

The two mice explained exactly what they'd been told by Barney the barn owl, and the policemouse wrote everything down carefully in his notebook.

'Good,' he said, as he tucked the notebook back into his

pocket. Then he looked thoughtful. Tiggy and Doris waited.

After a while he said, 'I have a plan. I'll tell you what it is but you must promise to keep it secret.' He then began to whisper and, as he spoke to the two mice, their eyes grew wider and wider.

'Do you think that will catch him?' asked Doris.

'Certainly, madam,' PC Catchem replied. 'Tomorrow, I will hide in the back room and we will put our plan into action. Not a word to anyone about it. Not one word. See you in the morning. Goodbye.'

When he had gone, the two mice closed the shop and set to work to prepare the secret plan, just as the policemouse had told them. At five o'clock, everything was ready. They locked the shop door and went home, wondering just what tomorrow would bring.

Once again, Tiggy arrived at the shop bright and early the next morning.

'I do feel a little nervous today,' said Doris when she saw her.

'No need to be nervous,' said Tiggy. 'PC Catchem will be hidden in the back of the shop and will be ready to pounce when the time is right. Let's put the rack outside as he said.'

This time there was a difference. Yesterday, the rack had been full of brightly coloured coats. Today, there was just one coat and it was the very best in the whole collection.

The two mice went back into the shop and waited. Several customers came in and bought a few things. A rabbit bought a lovely pair of red braces. A small mouse bought a sandwich box to pack his lunch in. Then PC Catchem arrived and, after he had greeted Tiggy and Doris, he hid himself in the back room.

At ten o'clock, they heard Barney give a hoot from his lookout post at the top of the tree. Barney had stayed awake even though it was long past his bedtime.

'Here he comes,' said Doris. Then she gave two knocks on the storeroom door to let PC Catchem know that it might be time for him to leap into action.

As they peeped through the window, they saw the grey squirrel sauntering slowly towards the shop. He stopped by the smart coat.

'That looks nice,' he said to himself. 'I think I'll try it on.'

'The plot is working,' whispered Doris to Tiggy, as she saw the squirrel wriggle into the coat.

'Shush,' Tiggy whispered back. 'We don't want to disturb him.'

The squirrel turned towards the window to admire himself, and the two mice quickly hid behind the honey jars. Alas, the squirrel saw them and, quick as a flash, without removing the coat, he ran for all his worth down the road.

'Constable Catchem!' shouted Tiggy excitedly. 'Quick, he's running away!'

PC Catchem came out of the back room and shot outside just in time to see the naughty squirrel disappearing as fast as he could. Then, he suddenly seemed to slow down and, before anyone knew what was happening, he was flying backwards towards the shop at a terrific speed. He was travelling so fast, in fact, that he bumped into PC Catchem and knocked him over.

The squirrel quickly picked himself up and set off again but, as before, he had only gone a short distance when he suddenly stopped. There was a terrific 'TWANG' and he again flew backwards.

This time the constable was ready for him. He marched towards him, seized the squirrel's paws and put his arms behind his back.

'Got you, my lad,' he said. 'Now, what do you think you're doing?'

The grey squirrel was totally confused and couldn't understand what had happened.

'I was just trying on this coat,' he said.

'Then running away without paying,' added PC Catchem. 'Well, it's off to the station with you, my lad. You have a lot of questions to answer. Come on, now. Take off that coat and come quietly.'

As the squirrel took off the coat, he noticed something unusual. There was a little fastener sewn to the back. 'What's this?' he asked, with a puzzled look. Then he understood. Attached to the fastener was a long piece of elastic, the other end of which was tied firmly to the front door of the shop. That's why he couldn't escape! He could run only a short distance before the elastic became taut and then pulled him right back to where he started.

By now, a little crowd had gathered and everyone clapped as PC Catchem handcuffed the squirrel and escorted him in the direction of Cheesethorpe Police Station.

That was the end of stealing in the village.

Perhaps one day you'll hear what happened to the naughty squirrel but that's a story for another time.